Night Sky Dragons

For John and Ruth McIntyre

MP & EG

For Alice Nabarro

PB

Night Sky Dragons

Mal Peet and Elspeth Graham

illustrated by Patrick Benson

WALKER BOOKS
AND SUBSIDIARIES

LONDON · BOSTON · SYDNEY · AUCKLAND

The boy clomped across the yard in his heavy winter boots, scattering the fluffed-up and sulky chickens. He stomped up the steps to the walkway that ran inside the high walls of the han. He climbed the ladder that rose to the rampart above the huge wood and iron gates and squinted out at the world. His face was small under the felt cap and above the collar of his goatskin coat. It looked like a fingertip poking through a hole in a glove.

The watchmen smiled when they greeted him. "Ho, Yazul! You're up early. You expecting someone?"

The low red sun spilled light into the valley and painted purple shadows on the endless, snow-smothered mountains that surrounded it.

"No," Yazul said. "I thought perhaps spring might have come."

The taller watchman shook his head. "No, not yet, Yazul. It's late this year. But soon. I can almost smell it."

The han stood in its valley halfway between the two ends of the world. In one direction, far, far beyond the sunrise, were the lands of the Great Emperor. That was where all wonderful things came from. In the other direction, far, far beyond the sunset, was the Great City. That was where the wonderful things were put on ships which sailed beyond the limits of Yazul's imagination.

Within the han's high walls travellers and merchant caravans found shelter. A place to rest and trade. A place of safety, too.

Between the ends of the world there were many dangers.

Yazul sniffed the sharp air.

When spring came, it would come with magical swiftness.
It would bring streams of clear, cold water, snow-melt from
the hills. It would bring the warm winds that are perfect for
kite-flying.

Soon. But not yet.

Yazul sighed, and shivered. He would go and see if his
grandfather was awake.

In Grandfather's workshop the fire was already crackling inside the brick stove. Later, it would melt a potful of thick yellow glue; but for now it warmed the tea-kettle.

"Pour yourself a bowl," Grandfather said. "The cold has turned your nose white." He smiled, and when he smiled the blue bird tattooed on his cheek shrugged its wings. This was one of the many reasons Yazul loved him.

Through the tea steam rising from the bowl Yazul looked around the workshop. Long stems of bamboo. Shelves of clay pots containing paint and ink and dye. Rolls of silk on wooden rods. Fat balls of twine. Sheets of precious paper. The tools and brushes laid out in the proper order. This room was Yazul's favourite place, the safest place in his small world. Here, after his mother died, his grandfather had taught him, patiently, the art of building kites and, out in the valley, the skill of flying them. Gradually, Yazul had discovered that the kites could lift his sadness into the sky, where little by little the wind would carry it away.

Hanging from the workshop ceiling was the hawk kite Yazul and his grandfather had worked on yesterday. They'd spent the whole day steaming and shaping the bamboo into a pair of broad wings and a tail like a fan.

Grandfather finished his tea and went to the rolls of silk. He rubbed his hands. He said, "Now then. What colour is our hawk, Yazul? Black? Orange?"

"Blue," Yazul said. "Blue like the sky in spring."

When the kite was finished, Yazul took it to show his father. His father was the lord of the han. Loneliness had made him stern, so although Yazul loved him he also feared him, a little. Yazul displayed the kite proudly.

"A fine kite," his father said.

Yazul smiled.

"Another fine kite," his father said. His voice was cold. Yazul's smile froze on his face. His father went to the window and stared out at the empty valley. "One day I will die, Yazul. Then this han will be yours to protect. And all the people in it. You will need to be a man, and strong."

Yazul did not know what to say, so he said nothing.

His father turned to face him. "Business, Yazul. Business. Money. That is the real world. That is food in your belly. That is warm clothes on your back. Travel and trade are what matters."

"Yes, Father."

A silence fell between them.

It ended when his father said, "I respect your grandfather, Yazul. I knelt before him when I asked his permission to marry your mother. But now he is an old man, and old men have time on their hands. Time to daydream. Or to fly kites, which is another kind of dreaming. But you are young, my son. Too young to live in dreams. There is nothing in the sky. Put your feet on the earth. Do you understand what I am telling you?"

"Yes, Father. I understand."

Yazul returned to the workshop with a troubled heart. His father's love was a sad and heavy thing. Kites rode the air and made him happy. It seemed he could not have both. But he was too small for such enormous choices.

His grandfather said, "Did your father like the kite?"

"Yes. He said it was a very fine kite." But Yazul did not look at his grandfather as he said this.

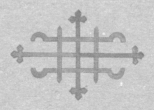

There was mischief in Yazul, a love of tricks. For example, he had learned that if you cut sections of bamboo in a certain way and put them into the fire of the stove they would explode. The air inside the hollow stems would swell in the heat and burst with a wonderful bang.

When he did this his grandfather would put a hand on his chest and cry, "Dragon! Save us, gods! Save us from the fire dragon!" Then he would slump onto the floor and pretend to be dead.

"It was me, Grandpa," Yazul would say, smiling. "Just me, not a dragon."

Then his grandfather would open one eye and the blue bird would shrug its wings.

But one day, not long before spring came to the valley, this trick went terribly wrong. Yazul was alone in the workshop. He was bored, so he went to the pile of unwanted bits of bamboo and found a nice thick one. He put it into the stove and shut the fire-door.

When the explosion came it was his best ever; the glue pot on top of the stove hopped. But it wasn't the bang that made Yazul whirl round. It was the crash and the scream that followed it. His grandmother stood just outside the workshop door, holding her hands to her face. Her eyes were shocked wide open.

"It's all right, Grandma," Yazul said. "It wasn't a dragon, it was…"

Then his voice died in his mouth because he saw what lay at his grandmother's feet.

A dish, a big one. Shattered into jagged pieces.

Fear filled Yazul like a winter sickness.

This dish was – or had been – no ordinary dish.
It was the history of his people. Coiling round its
edge and into its centre were delicate pictures
in blue and brown and white.
They told the story
of his ancestors.

The story of the old ones who had been
swallowed up by time. Their troubles and
travels, their marriages and great moments,
had been painted onto the dish. Many hands
whose bones were now dust had worked on it.
From his earliest childhood, Yazul had sat with
his grandmother while her old fingers traced the
tales and recited the names. His eyes had grown
wider when she pointed to the dragons that
appear in the sky when the gods are angry.
The dish was older than memory. It was his
grandmother's most valued possession. And now
Yazul's foolishness had destroyed it.

His grandmother turned and looked at him.
Her eyes were full of tears now, and her voice was
broken. "Yazul, Yazul. What have you done?"
He could not speak.

His grandfather appeared, his eyes full of anxiety. When he saw the shards on the ground his face turned to stone. He squatted and studied them.

Yazul made his voice work. "Can you mend it, Grandpa?"

"No," the old man said. "No, I do not think so."

His grandmother turned away from Yazul, then spoke to the sky. "It is a sign. Our family has come to its end."

"Nonsense," the old man said. "Superstitious nonsense. It is a broken dish and nothing more." But he did not look at his grandson.

Yazul's father's rage was as cold and fierce as a storm in the mountains. "It is idleness that has made you so foolish," he said. "Come with me." He led Yazul to the kitchens and summoned the cook. "This boy is your new drudge," he said. "Work him hard."

The kitchen servants did not dare mistreat or abuse Yazul. But they made sure he got the filthiest tasks, and grinned behind their hands while he laboured at them.

When spring came, Yazul did not smell it. Nor did he launch a kite into the rising wind. He was carrying buckets of slop to the pigs. When the melt-water tumbled into the valley, he did not hear it. He was raking ashes from the cook stoves, coughing. When the first caravans of the season arrived, he did not go with his father to greet them. While the courtyard filled with the neighing and bellowing of the pack animals, while their precious cargoes were unloaded into the han's strongrooms, Yazul was on his knees, scrubbing the kitchen's cold stone floor.

Weeks of slavery dragged by. Then, on an afternoon
when the sun was a white disc hanging in the sky, a shout
came from the ramparts of the han. "Caravan! A caravan
coming from the east!"

Yazul's father hurried up the steps and stared into the
distance, shading his eyes with his hand.

The watchman pointed. "There, my lord. Do you see them?
They're raising a lot of dust. They're moving fast."

"Yes. I wonder why they are riding so hard."

A cry from further along the wall: "Other riders, my lord! Away to the right!"

And yes, there was a second long cloud of dust moving along the higher ground, pursuing the hurrying caravan.

"Bandits, my lord?"

"Yes, perhaps," Yazul's father said quietly. He turned and yelled orders down into the courtyard. "Make ready at the gates! Archers, to your positions!"

The quiet afternoon was shattered by a clamour of shouts and frantic activity.

The caravan reached the safety of the han only moments ahead of its pursuers. The great gates slammed shut behind it, and the three massive iron bars that fastened them were heaved into place.

The courtyard was a chaos of men and animals. The travellers – merchants, their servants and guards – had faces masked by dust and streaked with sweat. Their long-haired and heavily-laden camels drooled ropes of foam from their muzzles. They were panicky, and did not know what to do with their huge feet. Their riders struggled to control them.

From the kitchen doorway Yazul and the other servants stared, wide-eyed, at the hubbub.

Up on the rampart, the lord of the han called out, "Do not shoot! Save your arrows!"

His archers relaxed their bow-strings. The bandits, perhaps fifty or sixty of them, had reined in their horses just beyond the range of arrow-shot. Fierce men with beards greased into rat-tails, swords sheathed on their backs, bows hanging from their saddles, quivers of arrows close to their knees. They sat silently on their horses, watching, while the dust settled around them. Then they slowly circled the han, studying it. Looking for its weaknesses.

Yazul's father walked along the walls, watching them watching him. He touched the backs of his men, steadying them.

When night fell, the bandits lit fires and rode in front of them, calling out taunts to the han. Offering its people choices of ways they might die.

Yazul's father called a meeting of the elders. "They will not attack us," he said. "They will lose men if they do. They will not shoot fire-arrows to burn us out, because the fire would destroy the things they want to steal. They will wait. They will hunt in the hills and drink from the river, knowing that we cannot. With so many new people in the han, we will soon run out of food and water. Their plan is to starve us into surrender."

"Yes," Yazul's grandfather said. "And what is worse is that other caravans will come here expecting shelter. Instead, they will be attacked. And when this becomes known, caravans from west and east will avoid us. We will have no way to live."

"True. So what should we do?"

No one could answer this question.

Many days passed, each one seeming longer than the last one before. The bandits waited, patient as wolves. Inside the han, camels and horses groaned their thirst. Hunger turned the people sullen and silent. At nightfall, they were tormented by the smell of meat cooking over the bandits' fires.

One morning, Yazul overheard his father talking with the steward.

"There is very little food left, my lord. We may have to start slaughtering the animals."

"The han is a place of safety, not slaughter," Yazul's father said sharply.

"Yes, my lord."

"And what about water?"

"The tanks are almost empty, my lord. If we don't get to the river in the next few days…" The steward's voice trailed away. His words dried up in the morning heat.

That night, after another hopeless meeting of the elders, in the darkness of the courtyard Yazul tugged his grandfather's sleeve. "Grandpa, I want to talk with you. I have an idea."

Yazul whispered into the old man's ear, then waited. In the dark, he could not see his grandfather's face. He could not see if the blue bird moved its wings.

"Hmm," his grandfather said at last. "It might work. Yes, it might just work. I'll go and speak with your father."

Yazul's father scoffed. "More foolishness, Father-in-law," he said. "More boys' games."

"Perhaps. But older and wiser heads have not come up with anything better."

The lord of the han grunted and stared moodily into the fire. "Very well," he said. "Now that there is little for him to do in the kitchens, it will at least keep the boy from mischief."

For three days and two nights Yazul, his grandfather and their helpers toiled in the workshop. The eight kites they built were bigger and stronger than any they had made before: taller than a man and wider than outspread arms. And black as a starless night. Black-dyed silk, black-painted bamboo frames, flying-lines blackened with ink. On each one the old man painted huge red

dragon eyes and red dragon mouths with ferocious teeth.

"Is this right, Yazul? Is this how you imagined them? Are they scary enough?"

"Yes, Grandpa."

"Good," the old man said. "They scare me." The blue bird on his cheek lifted its wings.

Each kite had a long, long tail of black twine soaked in oil. Threaded onto these tails were slender sections of bamboo the length of Yazul's hand.

"Will it work, Grandpa? Will they burn?"

"Hmm," his grandfather murmured, twiddling his beard. "I'm not sure."

Yazul waited anxiously while a long minute passed.

Then the old man went over to a cabinet in the corner and rummaged. "It's here somewhere," he muttered. "Is that it? No… Ah!" He came back to the workbench and set down a fat pot with a narrow neck and a tight stopper. Then he picked up a sharp spike with a wooden handle and began to bore a small hole into the first piece of bamboo on the tail of a kite.

"What are you doing, Grandpa?"

"This is my little addition to your plan, Yazul. Now, pass me that piece of paper. Yes, that one. Good. Now, watch."

The old man shaped the paper into a funnel and teased the thin end into the hole he had bored. Next, with a struggle, he pulled the stopper from the fat pot.

"A man from the East traded me this," he said. "I did not like him much. He told me that it would change the world, but I never found a use for it until now."

From the pot he tipped a pinch of brown powder into the funnel, tapping the paper with his finger.

"Pah," he murmured. "It stinks."

When the last grains of powder had trickled into the bamboo, Yazul's grandfather removed the funnel and sealed the hole with a blob of warm wax.

"There," he said. "Do you think you can do that?"

"Yes, I think so. But why, Grandpa? What is that stuff?"

His grandfather raised one eyebrow. "Aren't you Yazul? Aren't you the boy who loves tricks and surprises?"

When the last of the powder had been tipped into the last piece of bamboo on the last of the kite tails, Yazul's grandfather sat down, wearily. "I want you all to leave me now," he said. "I need to speak to the sky gods. I need to beg them for a dark night and a strong and well-shaped wind."

It seemed that the gods had listened, and been generous. That night, when the great black kites were carried silently up onto the walls of the han, not a single star peeped over the sky's dark blanket. The wind ran out of the west, strong and eager.

The bandits' campfires had burned low, now just yellow smudges in the darkness. The men on the walls waited until the only sound in the valley was an occasional snicker or snuffle from the horses. Yazul looked over to where his father stood, at the far end of the rampart, but it was too dark to read the expression on his face.

At last Yazul's grandfather murmured, "It is time."

It was not an easy task, launching the kites. As soon as they were lifted upright they strained to fly. It took two men to hold each one, and a third, bracing himself, to hold the handles of the flying-lines. The black silk hissed and rippled.

"Now," Grandfather called, hoarsely. "Release them!"

One kite failed to climb onto the wind. It tumbled, and dangled against the gates like a huge and wounded bat. The other seven soared, rising like black ghosts into the black sky. As they rose, the tails played out, the bamboo clattering softly against the parapet's stone floor.

"Catch those tails," Yazul's grandfather hissed, urgently. "Don't let them go!"

Yazul stared out towards the bandits' camp. Nothing stirred. No cries of alarm disturbed the night.

His grandfather scuttled along the wall, whispering questions and instructions. "Steady. Good, like that. Keep your hands level. Can you feel what the kite is telling you?
Is all the string reeled out?"

"Yes."

"Yes."

"By the gods, old man, it pulls like a bull."

"Good, good. Yazul – the burners."

Yazul picked up the two iron pots of glowing charcoal. He and his grandfather took each kite tail and held it in the embers, blowing breath onto them till the string caught fire. One by one, little worms of flame climbed into the sky.

For a short time which felt like a year, nothing happened.

"Let it work," Yazul prayed. "Please let it work." And then he clamped his hand over his mouth to stifle a cry.

Above the bandit camp a bright explosion
cracked and flowered. Then another. And as the fuses
burned from one bamboo firecracker to the next,
igniting the gunpowder, another and another.
The darkness was split by furious bangs and flashes,
and each flash lit up the red eyes and teeth of the dragons
hanging in the night.

Yells and howls of fear erupted from the bandits' camp.

"Dragons!"

"Sky dragons!"

"The gods have turned against us!"

Worse still was the terror of their horses. They pranced panic,
tore their tethers from the ground and raced, whinnying and
whirling, in all directions.

When the echo of the blast of the last sky demon faded,
the valley filled with a silence so deep that Yazul
could almost touch it.

In the first light of morning, Yazul's father led twelve armed men through the gates of the han and out into the valley. It was empty. Cautiously, they walked their horses through the yellow and white and pink flowers to where the bandits had camped. They found fire-beds of dead grey ash, abandoned bedrolls, discarded weapons, and seven black silk kites lying flat on the ground.

Yazul's father returned to the han and dismounted in the courtyard where Yazul and his grandfather stood waiting. He looked at his son as if he had never seen the boy before. Then he nodded, and his face opened into a smile. It was the first time Yazul had seen his father smile for a very long time. It was like the longed-for arrival of spring after a hard winter.

Then his father stooped and lifted Yazul onto his shoulders. Instantly, the han was a hubbub of cheers and shouts. Yazul's name echoed and re-echoed from the walls, and he was so full of happiness that he almost could not breathe. But even as he rode his father's shoulders around the courtyard, even as hands rose to shake his hand and slap his back, there was a part of Yazul's mind that was somewhere else. It was fixed on the difficult task ahead of him.

Authors' Note

For many centuries, the Silk Road was one of the most important trading routes in the world. It was enormously long. It went right across Asia, from China in the east to the Mediterranean Sea in the west. European traders carried wool and precious metals to China, and brought back rare and wondrous things such as silk and beautiful hand-painted ceramics. And gunpowder. Places of safety along the Silk Road were called hans. We thought that one of these remote places would be a great setting for a story.

We wondered if there might be a way to make a story involving silk and ceramics and gunpowder. And then we thought: kites!

Mal Peet and Elspeth Graham

First published 2014 by Walker Books Ltd
87 Vauxhall Walk, London SE11 5HJ

2 4 6 8 10 9 7 5 3 1

This book has been typeset in Columbus MT

Printed in China

British Library Cataloguing in Publication Data:
a catalogue record for this book is available
from the British Library

ISBN 978-1-4063-0985-0

www.walker.co.uk

It took almost a month of painstaking care, and when it was finished he was still not satisfied, even though he knew that it was the best he could do. He carried the dish to his grandmother and laid it on her lap. "I'm sorry," he said. "It is not perfect. You see, here and here?"

The old woman ran her thin fingers over its surface. Her lips moved silently.

Yazul waited.

"No," she said, "it is not perfect. It is better than perfect. Look here. Look closely." His grandmother's finger traced a pattern of cracks in the dish that Yazul's care had failed to conceal. "You see? It is a kite. You did not mean to make yourself part of this story, but you did. You will live in memory for ever, as the boy who saved us with his night sky dragons."